# WHEN I MET YOU

# WHEN I MET YOU

## A STORY OF RUSSIAN ADOPTION

ADRIENNE EHLERT BASHISTA

ILLUSTRATED BY CHRISTINE SYKES

DRT PRESS

*Thanks to Mom, Mark, and Ashley. You've helped me more than you know. —Adrienne*

Text copyright © 2004 by Adrienne Ehlert Bashista
Illustration copyright © 2004 by Christine Sykes
Cover and book design by Trish Broersma

For more information about DRT Press and books on adoption and families, please see www.drtpress.com or write to us at:

DRT Press, P.O. Box 427, Pittsboro, NC 27312

First Edition

The illustrations for this book were done in watercolor and pencil on Strathmore Illustration Board, 20 ply, cold press.

Printed in China

**Publisher's Cataloging-in-Publication Data**

**Bashista, Adrienne Ehlert.**
**When I met you : a story of Russian adoption / by Adrienne Ehlert Bashista ;**
**illustrated by Christine Sykes.**

**p. cm.**
Summary: A mother describes what life was like for her daughter before adopting her from Russia and what life is like for her now.
**ISBN 1-933084-00-6**

**[1. Intercountry adoption--Fiction. 2. Adoption—Fiction. 3. Adoption--Russia (Federation)--Fiction.] I. Sykes, Christine. II Title.**

**PZ7.B3**

**[E]—dc22**                                                                 **2004099562**

When my husband and I were in the process of adopting our son, Jamie, from Russia, we looked for a children's picture book about the special circumstances under which we met.

When we didn't find a book that fit our situation, I decided to create one.

This book is for Jamie and for the thousands of other children adopted from Russia and Eastern Europe each year. It's also for the hundreds of thousands, if not millions, of children in orphanages all over the world, in the hopes that someday they will meet the family of their dreams.

—*Adrienne Ehlert Bashista*

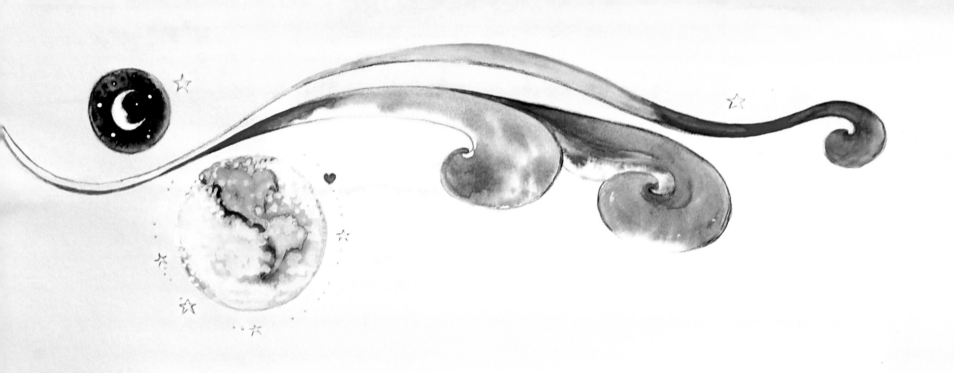

When I met you, you lived in Russia, a country far across the ocean.

Now, you live here, close to my heart.

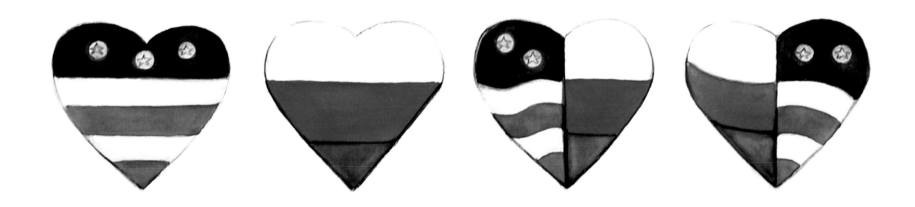

When you met me, you lived with a gruppa of sixteen other children.

Now, you live in a house, with me and Daddy and Fizz the dog.

When I met you, you were shy.

You wouldn't look me in the eye.

Now, your smile is open to the world,

and your face is full of love.

When you met me, you ate piroshki and kasha and sup.

Now, you eat peanut butter and watermelon and corn on the cob.

When I met you, from your window you saw city streets and tall gray buildings.

Now, out your window you see our backyard and the woods beyond.

When you met me, you wore heavy boots to keep your feet warm against the cold, cold winter. Now, you wear pink ballet slippers and pirouette across the kitchen floor.

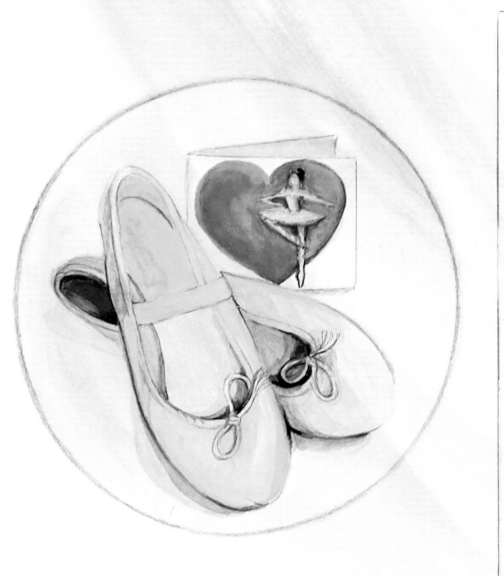

When I met you, you said "da!" "nyet!" and "spasiba!"

Now, you say "yes!" "no!" and "thank you very much!"

When you met me, you had a single tuft of hair on the top of your head.

Now, you have lots of shiny curls, and you grab my hand when I try to brush them.

When I met you, you slept in a room with crib after crib lined up against the wall.

Now, you sleep in your own room and you call Daddy and me when you need

us in the night.

When you met me, your Russian mother had already said good-bye.

Now, I am your mother, and I will say hello to you every day of your life.

You will always be Russia's child.

But now, you are also mine.

Can you find these images as you look at the pictures in this book?

Can you say the Russian words?

butterfly    **бабочка**
**ba**-boch-ka

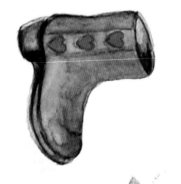

boot    **сапог**
sa-**pog**

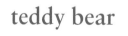

teddy bear    **мишка**
**m(i)ish**-ka

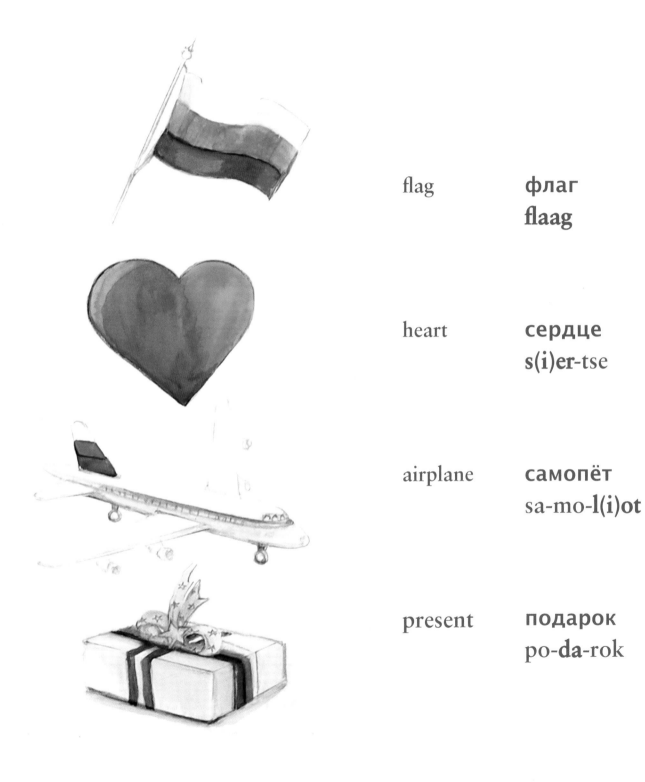

flag      **флаг**
             **flaag**

heart     **сердце**
             **s(i)er**-tse

airplane  **самопёт**
             sa-mo-**l(i)ot**

present  **подарок**
             po-**da**-rok

For more information about DRT Press and books on adoption and families, please see www.drtpress.com or write to us at:

DRT Press
P.O. Box 427
Pittsboro, NC 27312

To learn more about adoption from Russia, please contact Friends of Russian and Ukranian Adoption (FRUA) at
www.frua.org
and Eastern European Adoption Coalition (EEAC) at
www.eeadopt.org

*Adrienne Ehlert Bashista* is a writer, librarian, and mother to two boys. She lives in Pittsboro, North Carolina with her family. *When I Met You* is her first book. She wrote it for all the families created through adoption from Russia.

*Christine Sykes* has been an artist for more than twenty years. After receiving her Masters Degree in Illustration from Syracuse University, she began focusing her career on children's picture books. *When I Met You* is her first book on a subject very dear to her heart, adoption. It is her hope that this book encourages more families to open their homes and hearts to a child in one of the many orphanages around the world.